A BOOK FOR

Black-Eyed Susan

Written by JUDY YOUNG *and Illustrated by* DORIS ETTLINGER

SLEEPING BEAR PRESS
TALES *of* YOUNG AMERICANS SERIES

For Jordan,
who lives in what was once Oregon Territory

Judy

✳

For Mike

Doris

ACKNOWLEDGMENTS

Many thanks to my models, Sarah Wiessler and her parents,
Karen and Jeff, who helped me convey the affecting emotions of the story,
and also, to the Spolarich kids: Brian, Matthew, and Susan.

—Doris

Sleeping Bear Press™

315 E. Eisenhower Parkway, Suite 200
Ann Arbor, MI 48108
www.sleepingbearpress.com

Printed and bound in the United States.

10 9 8 7 6 5 4 3 2

Library of Congress Cataloging-in-Publication Data

Young, Judy.
A book for black-eyed Susan / Judy Young ; [illustration] Doris Ettlinger.
p. cm.
Summary: While traveling along the Oregon Trail, ten-year-old Cora and her
newborn baby sister suffer the loss of their mother and are separated, but Cora stitches
a book to tell the dark-eyed baby of their journey and family.
ISBN 978-1-58536-463-3 (alk. paper)
[1. Books and reading—Fiction. 2. Sisters—Fiction. 3. Sewing—Fiction. 4. Overland
journeys to the Pacific—Fiction. 5. Frontier and pioneer life—Oregon—Fiction. 6.
Oregon Territory—History—Fiction.] I. Ettlinger, Doris, ill. II. Title.
PZ7.Y8664Boo 2011
Fic]—dc22   2010028422

AUTHOR'S NOTE

Traveling on the Oregon Trail was not easy for the pioneers. There were many physical hardships, but there were emotional hardships as well. One that almost everyone faced was separation.

From their first steps west, the pioneers were separated from loved ones that stayed behind. Along the way, death also separated families and friends. Approximately one in seventeen died during the journey from illness, accidents, or in childbirth. Many children lost one parent, some both. It was up to other family members, friends, or even strangers to take care of surviving children, and sometimes siblings were divided among several families.

Near South Pass in what is currently southwestern Wyoming, the trail divided, separating those who had traveled together for more than 900 miles. Some took the California Trail with dreams of finding gold in that new state. Others continued traveling on the Oregon Trail toward the good farmland in Oregon Territory.

Once reaching Oregon Territory, education was a high priority and schools were quickly opened in the new communities. Teachers on the frontier were often young women who passed a test made by local school boards. One famous frontier teacher was author Laura Ingalls Wilder. Although Wilder never traveled down the Oregon Trail, she taught at a frontier school in Dakota Territory at age fifteen.

When writing historical fiction, research is used to support imagination so all that happens in the story could have happened, even if it didn't in reality. In *A Book for Black-Eyed Susan*, Cora and her family are entirely fictitious, but the events that happened to them were all possible.

It was still dark when Cora awoke. She looked across the prairie and saw her family's wagon glowing with lantern light. Yesterday Pa pulled their wagon away from where the others circled for the night, but told ten-year-old Cora to stay with Uncle Lee.

Cora ran through the tall grasses until she reached her wagon. Aunt Alma was inside holding a baby. Pa sat leaning against the wagon wheel, his head in his hands. Something was wrong.

"Where's Ma?" Cora could barely squeak out the words.

When Pa lifted his head, the lantern light fell across his face. Tears rolled down his cheeks. All he could do was shake his head and pull Cora tight to his chest.

When the sun lightened the sky, Cora and Pa stood side by side on a small hill. The others had already left the gravesite to get ready to move on.

"What about the baby?" Cora asked.

"Aunt Alma can take care of her," said Pa.

It was soon time to leave. Cora sat in the back of their wagon. Through her tears, she watched the wooden cross on the hill become smaller and smaller until it disappeared. Then, she lay down and cried herself to sleep.

The wagon bumped and jiggled across the prairie. Cora awoke when she felt its movement stop at noon. She climbed out and walked slowly to Aunt Alma's and Uncle Lee's wagon.

"Do you want to hold her?" Aunt Alma asked.

Cora sat down and Aunt Alma placed the baby in her arms. As Cora softly stroked the tassel of yellow hair on her sister's head, the baby opened her eyes. They were pitch-black.

That evening, Pa and Cora sat in front of the fire. They could hear Aunt Alma singing quietly to the baby.

"Pa," Cora said. "I have a good name for the baby."

"What?" Pa asked.

"Susan," Cora said. "She reminds me of black-eyed Susans."

"That's a beautiful name," Pa said. "Your ma would like that name, too."

"They were Ma's favorite flowers," said Cora, remembering how she picked handfuls along the trail for her mother.

The days rolled on just as the wagon train did. Cora helped Aunt Alma with Susan as much as possible. But one stormy day, Cora sat alone in her own wagon. As rain pelted on the canvas, she pulled out her mother's sewing box.

Thumbing through the scraps, there were many pieces she recognized. A piece from her Gramma's apron, one from Grampa's shirt, and another from Ma's favorite dress. Cora thought of the house they had left in Missouri. Gramma on the porch, Grampa leading the mules to the barn. She thought about Ma. Susan would never know any of them. She wouldn't even remember the trip to Oregon. Suddenly, Cora had an idea.

Cora took the scissors and cut squares, triangles, and rectangles from the scraps. She arranged the shapes on the largest square, threaded a needle, and started sewing. When she was done, she held up the square and smiled, remembering the farmhouse back in Missouri.

Across the prairie, Cora worked on different squares. One had a covered wagon. Another, a campfire with the cooking spider. Some had pictures of animals Cora saw along the way. Prairie dogs peeking from their holes, buffalo, a coyote, a hawk. There was a square with the strangely shaped cliff called Chimney Rock. Another showing a wagon crossing a river, and then mountains rising blue in the distance.

One evening Pa came to Cora. His face was sad, his eyes tired. He put his arm around Cora and without talking they walked away from the wagons. At last Pa broke the silence.

"I've asked Aunt Alma and Uncle Lee to raise Susan," he said.

"No!" Cora stopped, turning to face her father. "I can take care of her."

"You're too young," Pa said, "and a baby needs a mother."

"But they're going to California," Cora argued. "We'll never see her again."

"Yes, I know. We've gone through South Pass and tomorrow the train will divide up," Pa said. He sighed and shook his head. "This isn't the way I want things to be, Cora, but it will be best for Susan."

Cora turned and ran as hard as she could. Away from
Pa, away from the wagons, away from the baby. Finally
exhausted, she dropped into the grasses and stared back
east, toward her home a thousand miles away.

Cora knew, deep down, Pa was trying to do what was best.
Aunt Alma was already being a good mother to Susan.
But Cora didn't know if she could stand watching them
leave with Susan tomorrow. Suddenly, she jumped up.

"Tomorrow!" she said, "I've only got 'til tomorrow!"

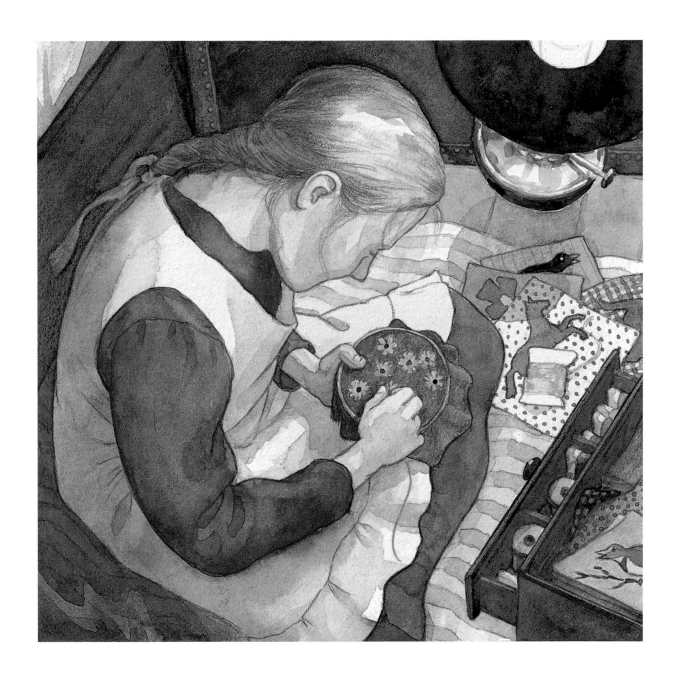

Cora raced back to the wagon and grabbed the sewing box.
She carefully embroidered a square until it was dotted with
black-eyed Susans. Then she took all the other squares she
had made and stitched them together. She smiled as she
leafed through them. It would be Susan's first book.

The next morning Cora rushed to Aunt Alma's wagon. Susan was sleeping. Cora gave her a good-bye kiss on the forehead and turned to Aunt Alma. She wanted to tell Aunt Alma about the book, but all she could do was push the cloth pages into her aunt's hands. Aunt Alma looked at each page and then wrapped her arms around Cora.

"I promise when Susan gets older, I'll give her this book, and tell her the story about how she crossed the prairie," Aunt Alma said. "And that she has a sister named Cora who loves her very much."

The wagon train divided. Cora and Pa moved on, crossing the high plains desert, then into the mountains, and weeks later finally reaching Oregon Territory. Soon Pa had built a home, and then a farm. A town grew up and a school was built.

Months passed into years. Cora did well in her studies and six years after she left Missouri, she took a test to become a teacher. It wasn't long before she was offered a position. A minister and his wife would journey south to open a new church and she would go with them to teach school.

"We have a few slates, but no books," the minister said as he showed Cora the schoolhouse. "We've asked the students to bring any they have from home."

"I've brought my old readers," Cora replied, setting them on the desk beside the slates. She also pulled out a ledger, a bottle of ink, and a pen. When the children arrived she asked them to line up in front of her desk.

"What's your name?" Cora asked the first child. She carefully dipped her pen and wrote his name in her ledger. She did the same with two more boys.

The next child stood in front of her desk. "And your name?" Cora asked, looking up from the ledger.

"My name is Susan, and I have a book."